CITY STORM

by Mary Jessie Parker

Illustrated by Lynne Dennis

SCHOLASTIC INC.

New York   Toronto   London   Auckland   Sydney

ISBN 0-590-42306-1

Text copyright © 1990 by Mary Jessie Parker.
Illustrations copyright © 1990 by Lynne Dennis.
All rights reserved. Published by Scholastic Inc.

BLUE RIBBON is a registered trademark of Scholastic Inc.

12 11 10 9 8 7 6   6 / 9

Printed in the U.S.A.   23

For Adela and Jennifer, with empathy
—M.J.P.

For Jean Maurice
—L.D.

Sun shines.

Vendors call.
People rush.
Children tug.

Clouds form.
Skies darken.

Rumblings sound.

Winds lash.
Hats sail.
Litter swirls.

Children cling.
Parents comfort.

Raindrops splash.
Vendors pack.

Umbrellas open.
Windows close.

Clouds race.
Lightning flashes.
Thunder crashes.

People scurry.

Rain pours.
People huddle.

They wait.

Lightning flares.
Thunder roars.
Dogs hide.

Birds tremble.

Leaves float.
Drains clog.

Tires splash.
Wipers slap.

Headlights shine.

Thunder rumbles.
Showers slow.

Sun peeks.
Skies clear.

Windows open.
Umbrellas close.

Dogs shake.
Birds bathe.

Vendors call.
People rush.
Children tug.

Rainbow glows.